FARMS

Verna Fisher

Nomad Press
A division of Nomad Communications
10 9 8 7 6 5 4 3 2 1
Copyright © 2011 by Nomad Press.
All rights reserved.

This book was manufactured by
Regal Printing Limited in China
June 2011, Job #1105033
ISBN: 978-1-936313-59-4

Illustrations by Andrew Christensen
Educational Consultant, Marla Conn

Questions regarding the ordering of this book should be addressed to
Independent Publishers Group
814 N. Franklin St.
Chicago, IL 60610
www.ipgbook.com

Nomad Press
2456 Christian St.
White River Junction, VT 05001
www.nomadpress.net

Contents

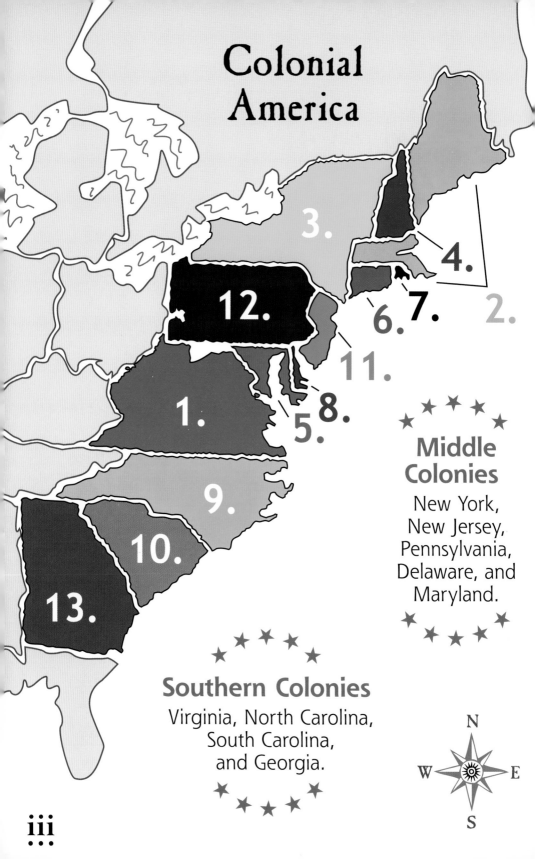

Colonial America

3.

4.

2.

12.

6. 7.

11.

1.

5. 8.

9.

★ ★ ★ ★
★   ★
Middle Colonies
New York,
New Jersey,
Pennsylvania,
Delaware, and
Maryland.
★   ★
★ ★ ★ ★

10.

13.

★ ★ ★ ★
★   ★
Southern Colonies
Virginia, North Carolina,
South Carolina,
and Georgia.
★   ★
★ ★ ★

N
W ✦ E
S

New England

Massachusetts,
New Hampshire, Connecticut,
and Rhode Island.

In the 1600s, people began leaving Europe to settle in America. Some were explorers searching for gold, while others came looking for freedom.

Jamestown in Virginia and Plymouth in Massachusetts were two of the earliest settlements where these people came to start a new life.

1607

1. **Virginia**

2. Massachusetts

3. New York

4. **New Hampshire**

5. **Maryland**

6. **Connecticut**

7. **Rhode Island**

8. **Delaware**

9. North Carolina

10. **South Carolina**

11. New Jersey

12. **Pennsylvania**

13. **Georgia**

1733

Down on the Farm

In colonial times, most people lived in **rural** areas on farms. Farming was hard work. Farmers grew food for their families and to trade with their neighbors. They also raised animals, called **livestock**.

rural: in the country.

livestock: farm animals raised for food and other products, or to do work.

colonist: a person who came to settle America.

crop: a plant grown for food.

Words to Know

The **colonists** did not have tractors or other machines. They had to plant **crops** by hand or with the help of livestock.

The New England colonists grew corn and apples. They grew pumpkins for pies, puddings, and breads. Those living near rivers and oceans caught and traded fish. Sheep farmers traded wool, thread, and fabric.

The Middle Colonies were called the breadbasket of **Colonial America**. The colonists grew lots of grain for bread there.

In the Southern Colonies, tobacco, cotton, and rice were important crops. **Plantations** in the south were much larger than farms in the north. People brought from Africa worked as **slaves** in the plantation fields.

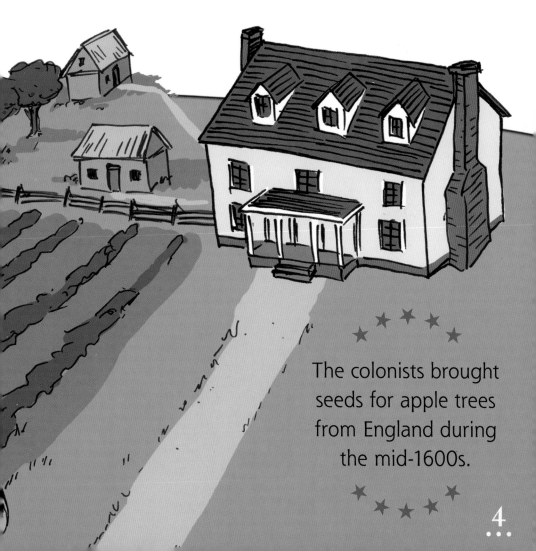

The colonists brought seeds for apple trees from England during the mid-1600s.

tend: to take care of something.

cabin: a small wooden house.

Words to Know

Slaves had many jobs on colonial plantations. They were expected to work long days in all types of weather. They **tended** tobacco, rice, and other crops. Slaves cleared land and built fences.

On smaller farms, slaves might work in the fields with the farmer. Here they were often treated better.

Large plantations had hundreds of slaves. This meant that slaves did not know their owners well and were often treated poorly. The slaves lived in small, crowded **cabins**. Sometimes they had little to eat.

A Day on a Colonial Farm

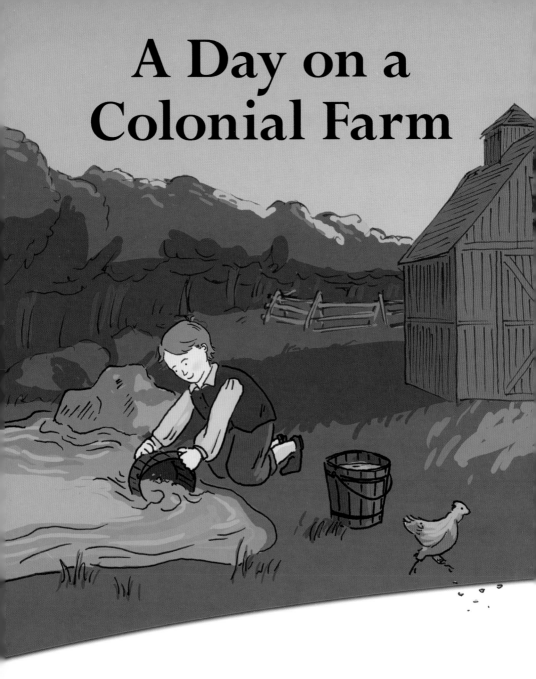

The day began early on the farm. Everyone worked from **dawn** to **dusk**. After feeding the chickens and milking the cows, children took the animals to **graze** in the **pasture**.

dawn: first light in the morning.

dusk: just before dark in the evening.

graze: to eat grass in fields.

pasture: grassy land where animals graze.

spring: water that flows out of the ground.

Words to Know

Children used buckets to fetch water at the **spring**. All of the water used by a family had to be carried in buckets.

Then the children cleaned the animal pens. Boys helped the men. They hunted, planted crops, and fished. They weeded and fixed fences and roofs.

herb: a plant used to season food and for medicine.

oxen: cattle trained to do work, such as pull heavy loads.

plow: to clear fields by breaking up the soil.

preserve: to treat food so it can be stored without spoiling. Drying, salting, and freezing are ways to preserve food.

Words to Know

The colonists grew **herbs** and smaller vegetables in backyard gardens. Fields were for larger crops of corn, wheat, peas, and beans, as well as for grazing animals. Farmers used **oxen** to **plow** their fields.

Did You Know?

The fat from pigs was used to make soap. The fat from sheep was used to make candles.

Girls helped the women. They cooked meals. They **preserved** food for the winter. Spinning wool into yarn, weaving yarn into cloth, and sewing cloth into clothes were all jobs for women and girls. Other jobs included making candles and soap.

village: a small rural community where people live close to each other. Smaller than a town.

Words to Know

Although colonial children helped on the farm, they also knew how to have fun. They rolled hoops and flew handmade kites. Kids played games like leapfrog, marbles, hopscotch, hide-and-seek, and tag.

Did You Know?

Toys were home made. For example, dolls were made from apples, rags, and corn husks.

Sunday was the one day of the week for rest. It was a chance for families to go to church in the **village** and visit friends and neighbors.

Homes on the Farm

The first homes in Jamestown, Virginia, were simple, one-room buildings. They were made of **posts** and **beams** carved from logs. Roofs were made of **thatch** and floors were dirt. Sticks, straw, and clay filled spaces to keep out wind, rain, and animals.

post: a strong piece of wood stood straight up for support.

beam: a strong piece of wood laid across posts for support.

thatch: dried straw used to make a roof.

privy: a small building away from a house. It has a seat with a hole in it built over a pit.

Words to Know

Then and Now

In colonial times, people used an outdoor **privy** to go to the bathroom, even in winter.

Today, we have bathrooms with flush toilets in our homes.

Log cabins were popular in the Middle Colonies. They could be built quickly without nails. Metal for nails was expensive and hard to get. Walls were made by stacking logs. Notches in the ends of the logs held them together.

You can still see many plantation homes in the South today.

Plantation homes built in the Southern Colonies were large and open because the weather was hot. They had large front porches with columns. Porches sometimes surrounded a house to give shade during hot days.

Farm Animals and Products

The settlers came to the **New World**
on ships crowded with farm animals.
The first ships brought small animals
such as chickens, goats, and pigs. Cows,
sheep, horses, and oxen came later.

New World: what settlers from Europe called America because it was new to them.

Words to Know

The colonists worried that they might not find these animals in the New World. They needed the animals for eggs, meat, and milk. The larger animals also helped the farmers do work in the fields.

leather: a material made from the skin of an animal.

quill: a large feather dipped in ink, to use as a pen.

butter churn: a long handle with paddles in a wooden container. It was used to turn cream into butter.

buttermilk: the liquid left after churning butter out of cream.

The colonists used animal products in their daily life. Milk was preserved by turning it into butter and cheese. Sheep's wool was turned into thread and woven into cloth.

Animal skins were used too. The colonists made **leather** clothing, bags, buckets, and shoes. Feathers stuffed pillows and mattresses, and were used to make **quills**.

Did You Know?

Butter was made from the cream that rose to the top of milk. The cream was mixed for a long time in a **butter churn**. All of the mixing formed lumps of butter that separated from the **buttermilk**.

Native American Farms

There were many groups or **tribes** of Native Americans. They lived all over America for thousands of years before the colonists arrived. The Native Americans were skilled farmers. They taught the colonists how to grow and cook with corn.

tribe: a large group of people with common ancestors and customs. Today, Native Americans use the word nation instead.

moccasin: a Native American shoe.

Words to Know

After eating corn, Native Americans used the husks to make **moccasins**, sleeping mats, dolls, and baskets. They burned the cobs for fuel.

Native Americans were able to grow a lot of food on a small amount of land. They planted corn, beans, and squash together. This combination was called the Three Sisters. Beans grew up the corn stalks. The squash grew below. Its big leaves kept in moisture and kept out weeds.

Words to Know

hemp: a plant with strong fibers used to make baskets and rope.

sinew: a strong, thin band in an animal's body. It connects bone to muscle and was used as cord or thread.

Native Americans made baskets to carry food from the field or riverbank to the village. The baskets were made with **hemp** and **sinew**. Weaving the materials tightly made the baskets very strong. Many Native American nations still make these baskets today.

Here and There

Colonists built fences to keep their animals on the farm.

Native Americans believed that all creatures were equal. They let animals roam freely in the woods near their villages.

Glossary

beam: a strong piece of wood laid across posts for support.

butter churn: a long handle with paddles in a wooden container. It was used to turn cream into butter.

buttermilk: the liquid left after churning butter out of cream.

cabin: a small wooden house.

Colonial America: the name given to America when talking about the years 1607–1776.

colonist: a person who came to settle America.

crop: a plant grown for food.

dawn: first light in the morning.

dusk: just before dark in the evening.

graze: to eat grass in fields.

hemp: a plant with strong fibers used to make baskets and rope.

herb: a plant used to season food and for medicine.

leather: a material made from the skin of an animal.

livestock: farm animals raised for food and other products, or to do work.

moccasin: a Native American shoe.

New World: what settlers from Europe called America because it was new to them.

oxen: cattle trained to do work, such as pull heavy loads.

pasture: grassy land where animals graze.

plantation: a large farm in a hot climate.

plow: to clear fields by breaking up the soil.

post: a strong piece of wood stood straight up for support.

preserve: to treat food so it can be stored without spoiling. Drying, salting, and freezing are ways to preserve food.

privy: a small building away from a house. It has a seat with a hole in it built over a pit.

quill: a large feather dipped in ink, to use as a pen.

rural: in the country.

sinew: a strong, thin band in an animal's body. It connects bone to muscle and was used as cord or thread.

slave: a person owned by another person and forced to work without pay.

spring: water that flows out of the ground.

tend: to take care of something.

thatch: dried straw used to make a roof.

tribe: a large group of people with common ancestors and customs. Today, Native Americans use the word nation instead.

village: a small rural community where people live close to each other. Smaller than a town.

Further Investigations

Books

Bordessa, Kris. *Great Colonial America Projects You Can Build Yourself.* White River Junction, VT: Nomad Press, 2006.

Fisher, Verna. *Explore Colonial America! 25 Great Projects, Activities, Experiments.* White River Junction, VT: Nomad Press, 2009.

Museums and Websites

Colonial Williamsburg
www.history.org
Williamsburg, Virginia

National Museum of the American Indian
www.nmai.si.edu
Washington, D.C. and
New York, New York

Plimoth Plantation
www.plimoth.org
Plymouth, Massachusetts

America's Library
www.americaslibrary.gov

Jamestown Settlement
www.historyisfun.org

Native American History
www.bigorrin.org

Native Languages of the Americas
www.native-languages.org

Social Studies for Kids
www.socialstudiesforkids.com

The Mayflower
www.mayflowerhistory.com

Virtual Jamestown
www.virtualjamestown.org

Index